MOG
and Bunny

written and illustrated by
Judith Kerr

HarperCollins *Children's Books*

For Lucy and Alexander

Other books by Judith Kerr include:

Mog's Christmas

Mog and the Baby

Mog in the Dark

Mog's Amazing Birthday Caper

Mog the Forgetful Cat

Mog and Barnaby

Mog on Fox Night

Mog and the Granny

Mog and the V.E.T.

Mog's Bad Thing

Goodbye Mog

Birdie Halleluyah!

The Tiger Who Came to Tea

The Other Goose

Twinkles, Arthur and Puss

First published in hardback in Great Britain by William Collins Sons & Co Ltd in 1988.
First published in paperback by Picture Lions in 1991. This edition published by HarperCollins Children's Books in 2005

30 29 28 27 26 25 24 23

ISBN-13: 978-0-00-717130-9
ISBN-10: 0-00-717130-7

Visit our website at: www.harpercollinschildrensbooks.co.uk

Printed and bound by Printing Express, Hong Kong

One day Mog got a present.
"Here you are, Mog," said Nicky.
"This is for you. It's called Bunny."

Mog liked Bunny.

She carried him about.

She played with him…

and played with him…

and played…

and played…

and played with him.

He was her best thing.

When Mog came to have her supper,
Bunny came too.

Sometimes Mog thought
Bunny would like a drink.

But Bunny wasn't very good at drinking.
"Oh dear," said Debbie. "Look where
Bunny's got to."

And she put him on the radiator to dry.

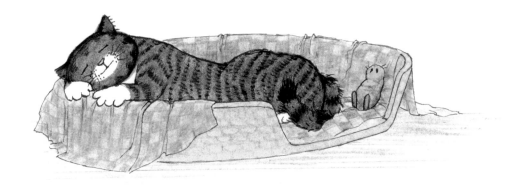

At night Bunny slept with Mog in her basket.

During the day, when Mog was busy,
she always put Bunny somewhere nice.
You never knew where Bunny would get to.

Sometimes Bunny liked to be quiet and cosy,

and sometimes he liked to be where there was a lot going on.

Mr and Mrs Thomas didn't understand this.
They didn't say, "Look where Bunny's got to."
They shouted, "Yukk!"

They yelled, "Arrgh! What a horrible, dirty thing!"

And they threatened
to throw Bunny away
in the dustbin.

One day Mr Thomas said,
"Let's have supper in the garden."

Everyone helped to carry things out of the house.

It was a lovely supper.

But suddenly…

...there was a crash of thunder and it poured with rain.

"Quick! Inside!" shouted Mrs Thomas. "It's bedtime anyway."

"Where's Mog?"
said Debbie.
"I expect she's keeping
dry under a bush,"
said Mrs Thomas.
"She'll come in later."

In the middle of the night,
Debbie and Nicky
woke up. Mog
hadn't come
in and it was
still pouring
with rain.

"Let's go and find her," said Debbie.

It was very dark in the garden.
They shouted, "Mog! Where are you, Mog?"
But nothing happened.

Then they heard a meow.
"There she is!" shouted
Nicky. "Come on, Mog!
Come inside!"
But Mog just went
on sitting in
the rain.

It was...

dripping...

off her nose.

"What's the matter, Mog?" said Debbie.
Then she said, "Oh dear! Look where Bunny's got to."

Nicky picked Bunny up
and showed him to Mog.
"It's all right, Mog," he said.
"We've set Bunny free.
You can come inside now."

Then they carried Bunny through the dark garden…

and through the house...

and they put him on the radiator to dry.

Then they all had a big sleep.

In the morning they told Mrs Thomas
what had happened, and how Mog had
stayed with Bunny in the dark and the rain.

Debbie said, "You won't really throw
Bunny away in the dustbin, will you?"
Mrs Thomas said, "No, never. It would
make Mog too sad."

Then she sighed and said, "Perhaps Bunny is not
quite so horrible, now he's been washed by the rain."
They all looked on the radiator.

But this is where Bunny had got to.